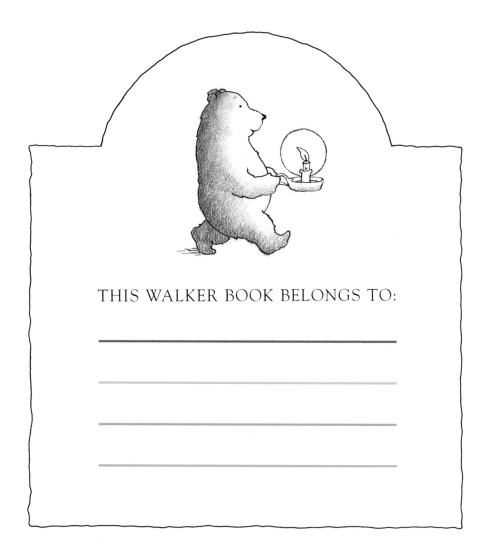

THIS WALKER BOOK BELONGS TO:

_____

To Pete, Caitlin
  and the Mighty Huffer

First published 1999 by Walker Books Ltd
87 Vauxhall Walk, London SE11 5HJ

This edition published 2003

10 9 8 7 6 5 4 3 2 1

© 1999 Bob Graham

The right of Bob Graham to be identified as author/illustrator
of this work has been asserted by him in accordance with
the Copyright, Designs and Patents Act 1988

This book has been typeset in Garamond Book Educational

Printed in China

British Library Cataloguing in Publication Data:
a catalogue record for this book is available from the British Library

ISBN 0-7445-9828-1

www.walkerbooks.co.uk

Buffy

An Adventure Story

Bob Graham

WALKER BOOKS
AND SUBSIDIARIES
LONDON · BOSTON · SYDNEY

Buffy had skills that were rare in a dog. As an assistant to Brillo the Magician, he did his job well enough… But Buffy had talents all of his own. He could juggle three clubs at once and throw a rope like a cowboy.

He could escape the
Houdini Deathtrap while
playing the harmonica.
"Bravo!" cried the audience.

His tap-dancing met with thunderous applause,
and how the dust rose from those well-trodden boards.

Brillo muttered darkly under his moustache.

Buffy was becoming more popular than him.

"OUT! and never come back," cried Brillo.

Buffy's bottom lip quivered with emotion
as he left the stage for ever.

He spent his last coins on a tin of dog food and a tin opener.

In a bleak railway yard he ate

the last of his Bonzo lamb chunks and pasta.

He wiped his mouth on his spotty scarf, and then …

Buffy jumped aboard
a moving freight train.

To the rhythm of the wheels,
he tapped his foot and sang,
"Oh, blue is me!
Oh, dearie me,
I'm as down as
A dog can be."

And while he slept, the train
continued its rhythm:
OUT, OUT …
and never come back.
OUT, OUT …
and never come back.

Buffy woke next morning to
the smell of fresh-cut grass
and countryside.

He put his harmonica in his
bag and leapt off the train.
"I will bring my tricks
to the world," he said.

But the world did not want Buffy's tricks. Nobody wanted a dancing sheep dog.

Nobody wanted a tiny rope-throwing cattle dog.

Nobody wanted a plate-juggling kitchen dog.

Nobody wanted
a guard dog
who played
the harmonica.

Only one person
wanted a wanderer
like Buffy …

but Buffy did
not want him!

"I will find myself a home," he said,
and travelled the world.

He sat above the roaring engines of mighty road trucks.

He crossed rivers,

and deserts.

He stood on
mountains and
moaned at
the moon.

Then one day Buffy stopped. He put down his bag,
wiped his brow and looked around him.

"I can go no further," he said.

"I'm not a sheep dog, a cattle dog, a kitchen dog
or a guard dog. So what sort of dog am I?"

"I am Buffy!
And I will do
what I do.
And this time,
the world shall
come to me."

Buffy's feet beat out the rhythm of the train on the tracks
and his harmonica howled like the desert wind and
pulsed like the engines of the mighty road trucks.

Many coins rattled into Buffy's cup that day and many faces passed by. Then someone stood in front of him. His breath stopped. His feet stopped. The sun came out.

It was Mary Kelly.

And Mary's mother   and her father   and her brother

and her grandma,   her grandad

and her baby sister,
Morag.

For Buffy, and the Kellys too,

it was love at first sight.

Off he went, the coins heavy in his cup.

At last, he had found a place to call home.

Now, each night after dinner, the music starts and each night the floorboards shake. Mary's and Buffy's feet beat to the rhythm of the jigs and the reels.

And Buffy lives up there, on the hill, to this day.

BOB GRAHAM says that *Buffy* is based on the life and times of his own dog. "We got him from a shelter; a victim of a broken home, we were told. And he told me the rest one day when he was sitting on a pillow in my workroom. He told me all of it, the whole story of his life. So it's all true!"

Bob has been writing and illustrating children's picture books since 1981. He has won several prizes including the Smarties Book Prize Silver Medal in 1999 for *Buffy*, and the Smarties Book Prize Gold Medal in 2000 for *Max*. *Queenie the Bantam* was Highly Commended for the Kate Greenaway Medal in 1998.